JO

# KATHLEEN GROS

# JO

*AN ADAPTATION OF*
## LITTLE WOMEN
*(SORT OF)*

## Quill Tree Books
Imprints of HarperCollinsPublishers

HarperAlley is an imprint of HarperCollins Publishers.
Quill Tree Books is an imprint of HarperCollins Publishers.

ISBN 978-0-06-287596-9—ISBN 978-0-06-287597-6 (hardcover)

The artist used Photoshop to create the digital illustrations for this book.

20 21 22 23 24  EP 10 9 8 7 6 5 4 3 2 1
First Edition

FOR C

# CHAPTER 1

I'M NOT GOING TO POST MY REAL NAME HERE, BECAUSE TECHNICALLY THIS BLOG IS A SECRET. JUST CALL ME "J." I'M 13 YEARS OLD, MY FAVORITE COLOR IS GREEN, AND TODAY I'M STARTING EIGHTH GRADE. I WANT TO BE A WRITER WHEN I GROW UP. THAT'S WHY I DECIDED TO START THIS BLOGJ.

I WANT TO SHARE STORIES ABOUT MY LIFE.

A NEW SCHOOL YEAR MEANS NEW BEGINNINGS AND FRESH STARTS. I KNOW I'LL BE SEEING THE SAME KIDS TODAY THAT I SAW LAST YEAR, AND THE YEAR BEFORE THAT, AND THE YEAR BEFORE THAT... BUT THIS YEAR THERE'S GOING TO BE SOMETHING DIFFERENT ABOUT US.

WE'RE EIGHTH GRADERS NOW.

JO! BREAKFAST!

I CAN'T SPEAK FOR ANYONE ELSE, BUT I KNOW THAT I CERTAINLY DON'T FEEL LIKE THE SAME "J" I WAS LAST YEAR...

COMING, MARMEE!

...AND I HAVE NO IDEA WHO I'LL BE WHEN THIS YEAR IS OVER.

publish

click

B IS TWO YEARS YOUNGER THAN ME. QUIET AND SHY, BUT VERY RESILIENT. SHE'S BEEN THROUGH A LOT, BUT EVERY DAY SHE'S GETTING STRONGER. SHE LOVES MUSIC AND HAS BEEN MAKING UP SONGS ON OUR LITTLE ELECTRIC KEYBOARD EVER SINCE DAD BROUGHT IT HOME FROM A GARAGE SALE YEARS AGO.

GOT IT, MARMEE.

AMY, PLEASE DON'T FORGET ABOUT YOUR CHORES.

MHMM.

A IS THE YOUNGEST OF US, AND KIND OF A HANDFUL--BUT DON'T TELL HER I SAID THAT! SHE LIKES TO STICK HER NOSE IN PLACES IT DOESN'T BELONG, BUT WE LOVE HER ANYWAY. WHEN SHE'S NOT CAUSING TROUBLE, SHE'S DOODLING ON ANY BLANK SURFACE SHE CAN FIND. DAD CALLS HER "LITTLE RAPHAEL" AFTER SOME FAMOUS PAINTER.

AND JO? DON'T STAY UP LATE READING UNDER THE COVERS.

I CAN'T HELP IT, MARMEE! IF I GET TO A JUICY PART OF MY BOOK, I'M NOT GOING TO BE ABLE TO SLEEP UNTIL I GET THROUGH IT!

WHEN M WAS A BABY SHE STARTED CALLING OUR MOM "MARMEE," AND BY THE TIME THE REST OF US CAME ALONG, IT STUCK.

WHEN MARMEE ISN'T TAKING CARE OF US, SHE'S TAKING CARE OF EVERYONE ELSE. SHE WORKS AS A NURSE AT THE LOCAL CHILDREN'S HOSPITAL.

MY FRIEND SUSIE WAS IN GREECE ALL SUMMER. SHE PROMISED SHE'D BRING ME BACK A SOUVENIR. I CAN'T WAIT TO SEE WHAT IT IS.

DAD LIKES TO SAY THAT THERE ISN'T A WOMAN IN THIS WORLD WITH A HEART BIGGER THAN OUR MARMEE'S.

AND I GUESS THAT BRINGS US TO DAD. HE'S FAR AWAY RIGHT NOW, DOING TOP SECRET STUFF FOR THE ARMY.

BECAUSE OF THE DISTANCE (AND THE SECRET STUFF) WE DON'T GET TO TALK TO HIM THAT MUCH. I CAN'T WAIT UNTIL HE COMES HOME . . . BUT UNTIL THEN, THANK GOODNESS FOR VIDEO CALLS!

HAVE A GREAT DAY, GIRLS! I LOVE YOU.

SO THAT'S US. MY FUNNY LITTLE FAMILY.

LOVE YOU TOO!

UNTIL NEXT TIME, I AM YOUR FAITHFUL BLOGGER, J.

I HOPE ANNA IS IN AT LEAST ONE OF MY CLASSES THIS YEAR! I'D JUST DIE IF SHE WASN'T!

I HAVE A FEELING THIS IS GONNA BE A REALLY GOOD YEAR.

YOU KNOW WHAT, AMY? ME TOO.

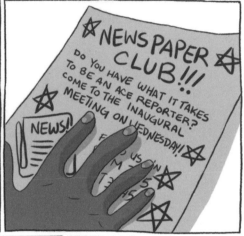

NEWS PAPER CLUB !!!
DO YOU HAVE WHAT IT TAKES
TO BE AN ACE REPORTER?
COME TO THE INAUGURAL
MEETING ON WEDNESDAY!!

NEWS!

HEY!

YOU SHOULD JOIN THE NEWSPAPER CLUB!

UH--

THE FIRST MEETING IS THIS WEDNESDAY AT 3:45!

IT WAS A LOT OF FUN LAST YEAR, AND WE'VE GOT SOME KILLER PLANS IN THE WORKS!

I DON'T KNOW...

shrug

WELL, THINK ABOUT IT!

YOU KNOW WHERE TO FIND US.

WATCH IT!

SLAM

HEY! YOU SHOULD JOIN THE NEWSPAPER CLUB!

DO YOU KNOW HER?

shrug

SORT OF.

SHE'S IN EIGHTH GRADE TOO, BUT SHE'S NEVER BEEN IN ANY OF MY CLASSES.

NEWSPAPER CLUB!!!

NEWS

MEG! MEG! TELL US ALL ABOUT HIGH SCHOOL!

WELL, IT'S BIG, AND THE SENIORS ARE KIND OF SCARY. BUT I'M SHARING MY LOCKER WITH ANNA . . .

AND JON IS IN MY HOMEROOM.

OOOH! JOOOON!

NOT JUST ME, BETH. THAT GIRL WAS INVITING EVERYONE IN THE LUNCH ROOM.

YEAH, BUT YOU'RE ACTUALLY A WRITER.

YOU SHOULD JOIN! THAT SOUNDS LIKE FUN!

I DON'T KNOW.

I LIKE TO WRITE, BUT I PREFER SHORT STORIES... AND BEING CREATIVE.

AND WRITING ABOUT MY LIFE.

DON'T NEWSPAPERS JUST WRITE FACTS? THAT SOUNDS SO BORING.

I'M NOT SURE I'D LIKE IT.

WELL, AS DAD WOULD SAY, "YOU NEVER KNOW UNTIL YOU TRY."

ha ha

I GUESS.

HEY!

YOU ACTUALLY CAME! I'M FREDDIE!

JO.

YOU LIKE TO WRITE, JO?

YEAH, I--

WELCOME! WELCOME!

WELCOME TO THE FIRST MEETING OF THE VOLCANO PRESS.

OUR SCHOOL'S FINEST, IF ONLY, NEWS RAG!

WHAT'S THAT?

THAT'S OLD-TIMEY FOR "NEWSPAPER."

IT'S GREAT TO SEE SO MANY NEW FACES!

AND A FEW OLD.

FIRST THINGS FIRST, LET'S DO SOME INTRODUCTIONS. I'M MS. DASHWOOD AND I'LL BE RUNNING THE SHOW.

WE HAD A GOOD RUN LAST YEAR, BUT I HAVE A FEELING THIS YEAR WILL BE EVEN BETTER.

AT THE END OF LAST YEAR, THE STUDENT EDITOR POSITION WAS LEFT OPEN WHEN TINA MOVED ON TO ROBERTS HIGH SCHOOL.

THIS YEAR, FREDDIE, ONE OF OUR LONGEST STANDING MEMBERS, WILL BE TAKING HER PLACE.

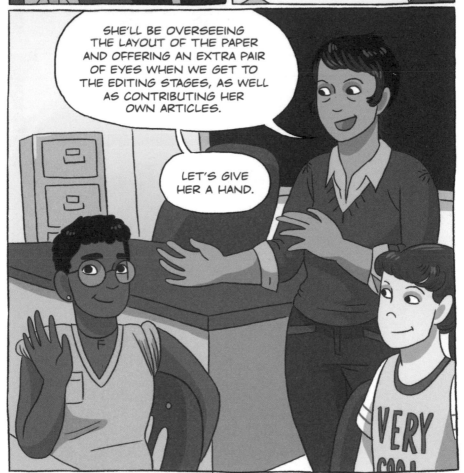

SHE'LL BE OVERSEEING THE LAYOUT OF THE PAPER AND OFFERING AN EXTRA PAIR OF EYES WHEN WE GET TO THE EDITING STAGES, AS WELL AS CONTRIBUTING HER OWN ARTICLES.

LET'S GIVE HER A HAND.

NOW, I'D LIKE TO MEET THE REST OF YOU.

TELL ME YOUR NAME, PRONOUNS, AND WHAT INTERESTS YOU ABOUT WORKING ON THE SCHOOL NEWSPAPER.

HI! I'M FREDDIE.

THIS IS MY THIRD YEAR AS PART OF THE NEWSPAPER. MY PRONOUNS ARE "SHE/HER" AND I LIKE EVERY ASPECT OF THE PAPER. FROM EDITORIALS TO HOROSCOPES--I'VE TRIED IT AND I LIKE IT.

I'M ALICE. I USE "SHE/HER" PRONOUNS. LAST YEAR I STARTED A FASHION COLUMN, AND THIS YEAR I WANT TO MAKE IT EVEN BETTER!

I'M TOM. "HE/HIM." IT'S MY SECOND YEAR ON THE PAPER AND THIS TIME, I'D LIKE TO WRITE AN ADVICE COLUMN.

TABITHA! "THEY" PRONOUNS, PLEASE. I'M NEW TO THE PAPER. I WANT TO TRY MY HAND AT DOING INTERVIEWS.

I'M SAM. "HE." MY GOAL IS TO EXPOSE THE SHOCKING TRUTHS HIDING IN PLAIN SIGHT.

FRANK. "THEY." FIRST YEAR ON THE PAPER. I'M REALLY INTO HOROSCOPES RIGHT NOW.

I'M SUMMER. "SHE" PLEASE. MY MOM THINKS THIS WILL LOOK GOOD ON MY COLLEGE APPLICATIONS.

HI. I'M JO. I USE "SHE/HER" AND I DECIDED TO JOIN THE PAPER THIS YEAR BECAUSE I WANT TO GET BETTER AT WRITING, AND TRY SOMETHING NEW!

GREAT! FOR OUR FIRST EDITION OF THE PAPER, I'D LIKE TO GET A FEEL FOR HOW YOU KIDS WRITE.

INSTEAD OF ASSIGNING TOPICS, I'M GOING TO HAVE YOU PICK RANDOMLY FROM A HAT.

REMEMBER! THERE ARE NO SMALL TOPICS. NO MATTER WHAT SUBJECT YOU GET, I WANT YOU TO TREAT IT AS IF IT WERE THE MOST INTRIGUING AND SENSATIONAL STORY!

VERY

School Lunches

SO WE CAN WRITE WHATEVER WE WANT, AS LONG AS IT'S ON THE TOPIC WE PICKED?

YES. I WANT YOU TO TELL ME SOMETHING NEW, SOMETHING I DON'T KNOW, SOMETHING INTERESTING ABOUT YOUR SUBJECT.

OUR CLUB WILL MEET EVERY OTHER WEDNESDAY IN THIS ROOM. NEXT MEETING WE'LL TAKE A LOOK AT SOME DIFFERENT FORMS OF JOURNALISTIC WRITING--HOPEFULLY IT WILL INSPIRE YOU.

YOUR FINAL PIECES ARE DUE AT THE END OF OCTOBER, BUT WE'LL DO SOME WORKSHOPPING BEFORE THEN.

THE KINGS, DOWN THE STREET, ASKED IF I'D BE WILLING TO DO SOME TUTORING ONCE A WEEK.

I GUESS KAT IS REALLY STRUGGLING WITH MATH, AND MINNIE NEEDS HELP WITH ENGLISH.

GOOD FOR YOU, SWEETIE.

MY HOMEROOM TEACHER THIS YEAR IS MR. DAVIS, AND HE'S BASICALLY THE BEST. THE GIRLS IN THE OTHER CLASS ARE TOTALLY JEALOUS.

WHAT'S SO GOOD ABOUT HIM, AMES?

WELL, FOR STARTERS, HE WENT TO ART SCHOOL BEFORE HE BECAME A TEACHER, SO HE UNDERSTANDS CREATIVITY.

HE SAID HE'S GOT A BIG ART PROJECT PLANNED FOR OUR CLASS.

THAT SOUNDS EXCITING!

WHAT ABOUT YOU, BETH? WHAT'S NEW IN THE WORLD OF SIXTH GRADE?

AM♥UR

UM.

WE GET TO TAKE BAND CLASS THIS YEAR. THEY ASSIGNED INSTRUMENTS AND . . .

. . . I GET TO PLAY THE FLUTE!

I DECIDED TO JOIN THE NEWSPAPER CLUB.

WE'RE GOING TO LEARN ABOUT THE HISTORY OF JOURNALISM, WRITE ARTICLES, AND PRINT EDITIONS OF THE VOLCANO PRESS!

WHAT A GREAT IDEA! YOUR AUNT MARCH WORKED ON THE SCHOOL NEWSPAPER WHEN WE WERE KIDS. IT WAS HARD WORK, BUT SHE LOVED IT.

I CAN'T WAIT TO SEE WHAT THE YEAR HAS IN STORE FOR YOU!

# CHAPTER 2

HI. ME AGAIN. J.

I SAID WHEN I STARTED THIS BLOG THAT I WANTED TO BE A WRITER, AND I DO, BUT LATELY I'VE BEEN WONDERING IF I'M CUT OUT FOR IT.

WHAT ARE YOU WORKING ON?

JUST THIS ARTICLE FOR THE PAPER.

WELL, LET ME KNOW WHEN YOU'RE DONE. I HAVE AN ESSAY DUE TOMORROW THAT I NEED TO FINISH.

WHAT IF I'M ACTUALLY NO GOOD AT ANY OF THIS?

I JOINED THE NEWSPAPER CLUB AT SCHOOL.

I THOUGHT IT WOULD BE FUN.

HEY! HOW'S IT GOING?

I GUESS I IMAGINED THAT BEING IN A ROOM FULL OF WRITERS WOULD BE COOL AND INSPIRING--AND IT IS.

ALL RIGHT.

I JUST DIDN'T IMAGINE THAT I'D FEEL SO USELESS AND OUT OF PLACE. M AND MARMEE, EVERYONE KEEPS TELLING ME I'M A GOOD WRITER, THAT I SHOULD BE ABLE TO DO THIS . . .

IT'S SO SHINY AND FLUSTERED!

DO YOU MEAN "LUSTROUS," AMY?

PLAY SOMETHING FOR US, BETH!

THEY SORT OF SHOWED US AT SCHOOL TODAY.

MAYBE YOU NEED TO BLOW HARDER?

I SOUNDED THE SAME WAY WHEN THEY GAVE ME MY TROMBONE.

ha ha ha

41

IT'S FRIDAY NIGHT, MARMEE'S WORKING LATE, AND YOU KNOW WHAT THAT MEANS...

MARCH GIRLS MOVIE NIIIIGHT!

WHAT ARE WE THINKING FIRST?

TNMS CHEERLEADING

THE CASTLE LAKE DIAMONDS, OR THE MYSTERY AT PLUMFIELD?

MYSTERY AT PLUMFIELD!

CASTLE LAKE DIAMONDS!

I'M NOT GOING TO SIT THROUGH THIRTY MINUTES OF YOU TWO ARGUING.

BETH, PICK A HAND.

TNMS

CHEERLEADING

WOO!

BOOOO!

43

I GUESS THAT PUTS AN END TO OUR MOVIE NIGHT.

NOW WE'LL NEVER KNOW WHO STOLE THE PLUMFIELD MANUSCRIPT . . .

YIPE!

BOOM

I'VE GOT AN IDEA. THERE ARE FLASHLIGHTS IN THE HALL CLOSET. I'LL GRAB THOSE. AMY AND BETH, GRAB ALL THE BLANKETS YOU CAN CARRY, AND MEG, TAKE THE CUSHIONS OFF THE COUCH. MEET BACK HERE IN FIVE!

IT'S TIME TO DISCOVER WHO STOLE THE MANUSCRIPT FROM PLUMFIELD MANOR.

BUT YOU HAVEN'T SEEN THE END OF THE MOVIE.

MAYBE NOT, BUT I CAN IMAGINE IT.

LATE ONE NIGHT, AFTER EVERYONE ELSE HAD GONE TO BED, LADY PLUMFIELD STOOD IN HER HUSBAND'S STUDY . . .

click

flicker flicker

...NEVER TO BE HEARD FROM AGAIN.

THE END.

GIRLS! I'M HOME.

DID YOU GET YOUR ARTICLE DONE?

IT TOOK ME FOREVER BUT YEAH, I DID.

SAME. IT TOOK ME A WHILE TO GET ALL MY RESEARCH TOGETHER.

I HOPE YOU'VE ALL PRINTED OUT COPIES OF YOUR ARTICLES!

TODAY WE'RE GOING TO BE DOING A BIT OF PEER EDITING.

FOR FUTURE EDITIONS, MYSELF AND OUR STUDENT EDITOR, FREDDIE, WILL BE HANDLING THIS STEP. BUT FIRST, I WANT YOU TO GET A FEEL FOR THE PROCESS.

EDITING IS JUST AS IMPORTANT A SKILL AS WRITING.

IT'S WHAT TAKES A PRETTY GOOD STORY AND MAKES IT GREAT!

I'M GOING TO PUT YOU INTO GROUPS OF TWO TO EXCHANGE YOUR ARTICLES.

WHEN YOU'VE READ THROUGH YOUR PARTNER'S WORK, I'D LIKE YOU TO TELL THEM WHAT YOU LIKED, AND WHAT THEY COULD IMPROVE ON.

REMEMBER, STATEMENTS LIKE "IT'S BAD" DON'T HELP ANYONE.

IF PART OF THE WRITING ISN'T WORKING, IT'S YOUR JOB AS PEER EDITOR TO HELP YOUR PARTNER FIGURE OUT HOW TO FIX IT!

OKAY, FRANK, WHY DON'T YOU WORK WITH TOM.

TABITHA, YOU AND SAM CAN PAIR UP.

SUMMER AND ALICE, YOU CAN WORK TOGETHER.

I GUESS THAT LEAVES JO WITH FREDDIE!

LET'S DO THIS!

## THE HISTORY OF DRESS CODES

### BY FREDDIE BHAER

EVERY YEAR WE GET SENT HOME WITH A LETTER TO OUR PARENTS BREAKING DOWN THE FINER DETAILS OF OUR SCHOOL'S DRESS CODE. EVERY YEAR SOMEONE, INEVITABLY, IS TOLD THEY'VE VIOLATED THE CODE AND ARE ASKED TO CHANGE.

SOMETIMES, IT'S BECAUSE THEIR SKIRT IS TOO SHORT. SOMETIMES IT'S BECAUSE THEIR TANK TOP STRAPS ARE ONLY TWO FINGERS THICK INSTEAD OF THREE. EVERY YEAR I WONDER, IS THIS REALLY NECESSARY? DOES THE WAY WE DRESS AFFECT THE WAY WE LEARN?

I POLLED THE STUDENTS IN MY CLASS AND EVERY SINGLE ONE OF THEM SAID THAT THEY DIDN'T CARE WHAT THEIR CLASSMATES WORE. THAT GOT ME THINKING, WHERE DID DRESS CODES COME FROM? WHO DECIDES THEM? WHAT IS THEIR HISTORY?

## WHAT'S FOR LUNCH?

### BY JO MARCH

LUNCH IS AN IMPORTANT MEAL. IT'S WHAT GETS YOU FROM BREAKFAST TO DINNER. AT THOMAS NILES MIDDLE SCHOOL OUR CAFETERIA HAS MANY OPTIONS, IF YOU DON'T BRING A LUNCH FROM HOME.

THE MENU ROTATES DIFFERENT OPTIONS THROUGHOUT THE WEEK. ON MONDAYS, THEY SERVE SLOPPY JOES. ON TUESDAYS, THEY SERVE PASTA. ON WEDNESDAY THEY SERVE HERO SANDWICHES. ON THURSDAY THEY SERVE MINESTRONE SOUP. ON FRIDAYS THEY SERVE PIZZA.

THERE IS A DIVERSE SELECTION OF DRINK OPTIONS, DEPENDING ON YOUR TASTES. THEY SERVE THREE TYPES OF JUICE: APPLE, ORANGE, AND GRAPE. IF YOU LIKE MILK, THEY HAVE BOTH REGULAR AND CHOCOLATE.

YOU DONE?

YEAH.

YOUR ARTICLE WAS SO INTERESTING, FREDDIE! I HAD NO IDEA SCHOOL DRESS CODES STARTED AS A REACTION AGAINST PROTESTS OF THE VIETNAM WAR.

OTHER THAN A FEW GRAMMATICAL ERRORS, I'M NOT SURE IF I REALLY HAVE ANYTHING TO ADD HERE.

THANKS! DRESS CODES SEEMED LIKE A TOTALLY BORING TOPIC, BUT ONCE I STARTED RESEARCHING THEIR HISTORY, I WAS HOOKED.

I WISH I'D SEEN YOUR ARTICLE BEFORE WRITING MINE.

TO BE HONEST, IT WAS HARD TO FIND SOMETHING INTERESTING ABOUT SCHOOL LUNCHES. THIS ISN'T THE TYPE OF WRITING I USUALLY DO.

WHAT'S YOUR USUAL TYPE OF WRITING?

AFTER TALKING TO YOUR PARTNERS, HOW MANY OF YOU FEEL LIKE YOU NEED SOME EXTRA TIME TO WORK ON YOUR ARTICLES?

GREAT! THAT MEANS YOU'RE DOING A GOOD JOB HELPING EACH OTHER. I'M LOOKING FORWARD TO SEEING YOUR FINISHED ARTICLES AT THE END OF OCTOBER.

THANKS FOR YOUR HELP, FREDDIE.

THAT'S WHAT EDITORS ARE FOR!

MEG, YOU SEEM A LITTLE DOWN TODAY.

IT'S THIS TUTORING.

I KNEW IT WOULD BE A CHALLENGE, BUT THE KING KIDS ARE SO SPOILED!

I CAN'T BELIEVE HOW MANY TIMES I'VE HAD TO TAKE THEIR PHONES AWAY . . .

. . . ONLY TO TURN AROUND FIVE SECONDS LATER TO FIND THEM PLAYING GAMES ON THEIR TABLETS!

YOU KNOW, MEG, IF THE PHONES AND TABLETS ARE DISTRACTING THE KIDS, IT MIGHT BE TIME TO BRING IT UP WITH MR. AND MRS. KING.

THEY WOULDN'T WANT THEIR KIDS WASTING THEIR TUTORING TIME, WHICH THEY'RE PAYING YOU FOR, WITH ELECTRONICS.

YEAH, YOU'RE PROBABLY RIGHT.

I-I CAN'T GET THE EMBOUCHURE RIGHT FOR PLAYING THE FLUTE.

I EITHER MAKE NO NOISE, OR IT SOUNDS LIKE A BANSHEE.

OH, WE KNOW.

MAYBE I SHOULD STICK TO PLAYING THE PIANO.

SIGH

BETH, IF YOU KEEP PRACTICING, I KNOW YOU'LL GET BETTER AT THE FLUTE. REMEMBER WHEN YOU STARTED PLAYING THE PIANO?

YOU STRUGGLED WITH SCALES AND KEEPING TRACK OF TWO HANDS PLAYING TWO SEPARATE MELODIES? AND NOW LOOK AT YOU. WITH TIME, YOU'LL FIND THAT THE FLUTE GETS EASIER.

WELL, I THOUGHT HAVING A TEACHER WHO LIKED ART WOULD BE GREAT.

BUT WE'RE NOT DRAWING ANYTHING FUN! ALL WE'VE DONE SO FAR IS DRAW BOXES AND VANISHING POINTS, AND LEARN RULES, RULES, RULES!

stab stab stab

WHY DO RULES EVEN MATTER? AREN'T THEY STIPPLING OUR CREATIVITY?

STIFLING, AMY. STIFLING YOUR CREATIVITY.

heh

THAT'S WHAT I SAID.

AMY, THE RULES OF DRAWING ARE THERE SO IT'S MORE FUN WHEN YOU GET TO BREAK THEM. BUT YOU HAVE TO LEARN THEM FIRST.

I TURNED IN MY FIRST ARTICLE FOR THE NEWSPAPER . . .

. . . AND IT WAS A FLOP.

BUT FREDDIE, THE STUDENT EDITOR, GAVE ME SOME ADVICE AND MS. DASHWOOD SAID WE COULD HAVE MORE TIME TO WORK ON IT. SO I THINK I HAVE A GOOD IDEA HOW TO MAKE IT BETTER.

MOST THINGS AREN'T EASY ON THE FIRST TRY.

USUALLY, IT TAKES A WHILE TO GET THINGS RIGHT.

MY FIRST YEAR OF NURSING SCHOOL, I WAS HOPELESS. I EVEN CONSIDERED DROPPING OUT AND DOING SOMETHING ELSE. BUT I KEPT AT IT, AND I'M GLAD I DID.

NOW, I THINK I HAVE SOME NEWS THAT WILL BRIGHTEN YOUR MOODS. I GOT AN EMAIL FROM DAD!

# CHAPTER 3

gobble
gobble gobble
munch

SLURP

slurp

slurp

APP

WHERE ARE YOU GOING?

ZZIIIIIIP

MY ARTICLE REWRITE IS DUE SOON AND I'VE STILL GOT A TON OF RESEARCH TO DO!

78

THE LEAVES ARE TURNING AND THE TEMPERATURE'S DROPPING. PUMPKINS ARE SHOWING UP ON PEOPLE'S DOORSTEPS. HALLOWEEN IS IN THE AIR! I LOVE GETTING DRESSED UP AND PRETENDING TO BE SOMEONE ELSE FOR THE DAY!

SNIP SNIP

THIS YEAR I'M GOING AS A VAMPIRE. MARMEE DOESN'T BELIEVE IN BUYING COSTUMES--SHE INSISTS IT'S BETTER IF WE MAKE THEM. M HELPED ME SEW A CAPE FROM ONE OF MARMEE'S OLD DRESSES, AND A SAYS SHE CAN MAKE KILLER FAKE BLOOD OUT OF CORN SYRUP AND FOOD DYE.

M'S GOING TO BE A WITCH, WHICH IS BASICALLY THE EASIEST COSTUME TO MAKE. I GUESS SHE AND HER FRIENDS ARE GOING TO BE A COVEN. A MADE HER A HAT FROM PAPER IN OUR CRAFT SUPPLY STASH.

TIMID *B* HAS DECIDED TO BE A MOUSE. MARMEE'S MADE HER EARS AND A TAIL OUT OF LEFTOVER FELT.

*A* HAS SPENT WEEKS COPYING DA VINCI'S MASTERPIECE ONTO CARDBOARD--SHE'S GOING AS THE MONA LISA, AND IF THAT DOESN'T TELL YOU WHAT TYPE OF PERSON *A* IS, I DON'T KNOW WHAT WILL.

I THINK WHO WE PRETEND TO BE SAYS A LOT ABOUT WHO WE ARE. BUT I'LL LET YOU DRAW YOUR OWN CONCLUSIONS. I HAVE A DANCE TO GO TO.

VAMPIRICALLY YOURS,
**J**

HE THOUGHT THIS DANCE WOULD BE A GOOD WAY FOR ME TO MEET MY CLASSMATES.

I TOLD HIM SCHOOL WOULD PROBABLY BE BETTER FOR THAT, BUT HE DIDN'T GIVE ME MUCH OF A CHOICE.

I START AT THOMAS NILES MIDDLE SCHOOL ON MONDAY.

I THINK GRANDPA SAID MY HOMEROOM TEACHER'S NAME WAS MRS. BRONSON?

I'M IN HER CLASS! SHE TEACHES HOMEROOM AND SCIENCE.

I FEEL A LOT LESS NERVOUS WITH SOMEONE I KNOW IN THE CLASS.

I CAN GIVE YOU ALL THE INSIDER INFO!

SO, JO, GIVE ME THE SCOOP ON THIS DANCE!

I'M ONLY HERE BECAUSE MY SISTER BEGGED ME TO COME WITH HER.

I'M BASICALLY HER MORAL SUPPORT. DANCES AREN'T REALLY MY THING.

SO YOU'VE GOT A SISTER?

I'VE GOT THREE.

THREE!?

YEAH. BUT IT'S JUST ME AND MEG HERE TONIGHT.

SHE'S OVER THERE DANCING WITH HER CRUSH, JON. HE PLAYS ON THE HIGH SCHOOL FOOTBALL TEAM.

...BUT THE REST OF THE TIME, I LOVE THEM.

WHAT ABOUT YOU? DO YOU HAVE ANY SIBLINGS?

NO, I'M AN ONLY CHILD.

SEE, I CAN'T IMAGINE THAT.

UM. DO YOU WANT TO DANCE? I FEEL SORT OF WEIRD BEING THE ONLY ONES SITTING OUT.

IF YOU VALUE YOUR LIFE YOU WILL FIND ANOTHER DANCE PARTNER, LAURIE.

I DON'T WANT TO BRAG, BUT I'VE CAUSED MORE INJURIES ON THE DANCE FLOOR THAN SHOULD BE HUMANLY POSSIBLE.

TRUST ME, BOARDING SCHOOL REALLY ISN'T AS EXCITING AS YOU'RE IMAGINING.

MY PARENTS TRAVEL ALL OVER THE WORLD FOR WORK.

WHEN I WAS REALLY LITTLE THEY TOOK ME WITH THEM, BUT THEN THEY CHANGED THEIR MINDS ABOUT THAT AND DECIDED IT WOULD BE LESS DISRUPTIVE TO SEND ME TO BOARDING SCHOOL.

AND NOW THEY'VE CHANGED THEIR MINDS ABOUT THAT SO I'M LIVING WITH MY GRANDPA AND ENROLLED IN PUBLIC SCHOOL.

JEEZ!

WELL, HERE WE ARE!

THIS IS **YOUR** HOUSE!? I DON'T BELIEVE IT!

WHAT DO YOU MEAN?

THE FIRST PEOPLE I MEET AT THE DANCE . . . AND IT TURNS OUT WE'RE NEIGHBORS!

YOUR GRANDPA
IS OLD MR. LAURENCE!?

UH-HUH.

nod

LAURIE
LAURENCE.

DID YOUR
PARENTS DO THAT
ON PURPOSE?

OF COURSE NOT!
LAURIE'S A NICKNAME.
BUT I'M NOT TELLING YOU
MY FIRST NAME BECAUSE
YOU'LL JUST MAKE FUN
OF ME.

NO! WE
WOULDN'T!

AT LEAST
GIVE US
A HINT!

NO WAY.
THAT SECRET DIES
WITH ME.

97

HMM . . .

LOOKS LIKE IT'S NOTHING SERIOUS.

A BIT OF ICE AND STAYING OFF IT IS ALL IT NEEDS.

I'LL GET SOME ICE!

AND WHO ARE YOU?

LAURIE, MA'AM. I THINK YOU KNOW MY GRANDPA, YOUR NEIGHBOR, JAMES LAURENCE?

JO MADE A *FRIEND* AT THE DANCE.

OH, OF COURSE! YOUR GRANDPA MENTIONED YOU'D BE COMING TO STAY.

I'D OFFER YOU SOME CANDY, BUT THE TRICK-OR-TREATERS HAVE COMPLETELY CLEANED ME OUT.

AHHH!

THAT FEELS SO MUCH BETTER.

SLAM!

THE KINGS WERE GIVING OUT FULL-SIZE CANDY BARS THIS YEAR!

# CHAPTER 4

IT'S WHAT MAKES
ENERGY FOR THE CELL.

I LIKED IT TOO! I CAN'T WAIT TO SEE WHAT YOU WRITE NEXT.

## What's for Lunch?
By Jo March

Here at Thomas Niles, everyone can agree that lunch is an important meal. It's what gets you from breakfast to dinner. It's where you get to socialize and hang out with friends in between classes. We trade food and trade jokes. Whether you bring your lunch from home, or buy it in our cafeteria, everyone has something that's their favorite. A few weeks ago, I spent my lunch period finding out exactly what those favorites are. In the staff room, salad seems to reign supreme. What else would you expect from a bunch of adults? Mr. Charles, the janitor, says that he likes to add roasted chickpeas to his salads for crunch and protein. In the cafeteria, it's a solid tie between pizza lunch Fridays and whoever's mom packed cookies today...

HELLO, DEAR READERS, (IF YOU'RE STILL FOLLOWING ALONG).

THERE'S THAT SAYING THAT GOES "IF AT FIRST YOU DON'T SUCCEED, TRY, TRY, AGAIN."

OH! THAT'S YOU!

IT'S SAPPY, AND I ALWAYS THOUGHT IT SOUNDED KIND OF SILLY, BUT I GUESS THERE'S SOME TRUTH TO IT. I DIDN'T DO GREAT WITH MY FIRST ARTICLE FOR THE NEWSPAPER, BUT WHEN I REWROTE IT, I CAME UP WITH SOMETHING NEW AND, I'M TOLD, VASTLY IMPROVED.

M, B, AND A HAVE ALL KEPT GOING AT THE THINGS THAT THEY WERE STRUGGLING WITH. M'S TUTEES ARE DOING BETTER THAN EVER.

B HAS FINALLY FIGURED OUT HOW TO PLAY NOTES ON HER FLUTE THAT DON'T SOUND LIKE THE SHRIEKS OF A BANSHEE.

Amy March

AND A HAS MADE PEACE WITH HER TEACHER AFTER HE TOLD HER THAT SHE WAS "REALLY GETTING" PERSPECTIVE.

WHAP

ACK!

he he he

LAURIE!

WHOOSH

ACK!

PAF

AUGH!

PAF
PAF
PAF

NO FAIR! THAT'S FOUR AGAINST ONE.

I SURRENDER.

ha ha ha

YOU'RE NO MATCH FOR THE MARCH GIRLS, LAURIE LAURENCE.

# CHAPTER 5

CHRISTMAS IS ABOUT TRADITIONS AND BEING TOGETHER AS A FAMILY.

BUT THIS YEAR, WITH DAD SO FAR AWAY, THE TRADITIONS SEEM HOLLOW.

IT FEELS WEIRD MAKING A FAMILY OF SNOW PEOPLE IN THE YARD WHEN OUR FAMILY ISN'T WHOLE.

IT'S NOT THE SAME PICKING OUT THE TREE WITHOUT HIM.

ONCOLOGY

WE CAN LEAVE THIS ONE FOR MEG AND AMY IF YOU WANT.

BETH MARCH! MY FAVORITE PATIENT!

143

THE FIRST CHRISTMAS YOUR DAD AND I SPENT TOGETHER, WE COULDN'T AFFORD MUCH IN THE WAY OF GIFTS.

AT THE TIME, WE COULDN'T EVEN AFFORD TO GO HOME AND VISIT OUR PARENTS OUT WEST, LIKE WE DO NOW DURING THE SUMMER.

CHRISTMAS MORNING FELT LONELY WITHOUT THE REST OF OUR FAMILY, SO WE DECIDED TO FILL THE DAY WITH FUN. WE SPENT THE WHOLE AFTERNOON AT THE SKATING RINK.

NOW, WHENEVER I PASS THIS RINK, EVEN IN THE SUMMER, I THINK BACK ON OUR FIRST CHRISTMAS AND HOW WE HAD SO MUCH FUN WHEN WE HAD SO LITTLE.

THAT'S SO ROMANTIC!

SO LET'S SKATE TODAY, AND THINK OF DAD. WHEREVER HE IS, I'M SURE IT'S NOT COLD ENOUGH TO SKATE. LET'S DO IT FOR HIM.

SKATE RENTALS

147

SHE'S RIGHT.

AMY MADE US ALL HATS THIS YEAR.

hm.

JUST WEAR IT. YOU DON'T WANT TO START THE NEW YEAR WITH THE WRATH OF AMY FOCUSED ON YOU.

ha ha    nudge

ARE WE READY FOR SOME CAKE?

YEAH!

WHAT WERE YOUR FAVORITE PARTS OF THIS YEAR?

SEEING MY NAME PUBLISHED IN THE NEWSPAPER.

DANCING WITH JON AT HALLOWEEN.

GETTING MY FLUTE.

WHEN MR. DAVIS TOLD THE CLASS MY DRAWINGS WERE "EXCELLENT."

MOVING IN WITH MY GRANDPA BECAUSE IT MEANT MEETING ALL OF YOU.

OH YEAH! THAT'S ONE OF MY FAVORITE PARTS OF THIS YEAR TOO.

HUG

# CHAPTER 6

JO, HONEY, PHONE'S FOR YOU.

HELLO?

YOU'RE WHAT!?

WELL, WHO AM I GONNA SIT WITH IN SOCIAL STUDIES?

AW, MAN, THAT SUCKS.

YEAH.

OKAY.

BYE.

WHO WAS THAT?

LAURIE'S GOT CHICKEN POX AND HE WON'T BE AT SCHOOL FOR AN ENTIRE WEEK!

POOR GUY. I'M GLAD WE GOT THAT OVER WITH WHEN WE WERE LITTLE. ALL THAT ITCHING WAS THE WORST!

I THINK I STILL HAVE A FEW SCARS. EVEN THOUGH MARMEE WARNED ME, I COULDN'T STOP SCRATCHING.

I COME BEARING HOMEWORK!

JO! IT'S GOOD TO SEE YOU, BUT NOW I DON'T HAVE AN EXCUSE FOR NOT DOING MY HOMEWORK.

Plop!

I THOUGHT YOU'D BE BORED, SO I ALSO BROUGHT SOME GAMES.

I HOPE IT'S OKAY BUT BETH AND AMY ARE DOWNSTAIRS. I THINK BETH ALMOST FAINTED WHEN SHE SAW YOUR PIANO.

SHE SHOULD PLAY IT!

I DON'T THINK ANYONE HERE DOES.

NOW WHAT DID YOU SAY ABOUT GAMES?

I'VE BEEN PRACTICALLY DYING COOPED UP IN HERE. I HAVEN'T LEFT THE HOUSE IN THREE DAYS, SINCE I GOT ALL . . . CHICKEN POX-Y.

GRANDPA'S ALWAYS AT WORK AND OUR HOUSEKEEPER ISN'T MUCH FUN.

MEG'LL GET MAD IF WE DON'T DO OUR HOMEWORK FIRST . . .

BUT WHAT SHE DOESN'T KNOW WON'T HURT HER.

HAVING CHICKEN POX SUCKS.

ESPECIALLY WITH MY MOM SO FAR AWAY.

BETH GOT REALLY SICK TWO YEARS AGO.

AT FIRST EVERYONE CAME TO VISIT HER, BUT THE SICKER SHE GOT, THE FEWER FRIENDS CAME BY. MEG, AMY, AND I, WE TRIED TO MAKE SURE SHE NEVER FELT ALONE, BUT I KNOW SHE MISSED HER FRIENDS.

I DON'T BLAME THEM, THOUGH. IT WAS SCARY SEEING HER LIKE THAT.

WHAT WAS WRONG WITH HER?

SHE HAD LEUKEMIA.

I HAD NO IDEA.

IT'S NOT A SECRET OR ANYTHING. IT'S JUST WEIRD TO TALK ABOUT, YOU KNOW?

"HI, MY NAME IS JO AND I USED TO BE REALLY WORRIED THAT MY SISTER WAS GOING TO DIE."

IT'S NOT GREAT SMALL TALK.

THE CANCER'S BEEN IN REMISSION FOR A WHILE, THOUGH. NOW SHE TAKES PILLS EVERY DAY TO KEEP IT FROM COMING BACK. ONCE A MONTH SHE GOES IN TO THE HOSPITAL FOR SOME SPECIAL TREATMENTS, BUT SOON SHE WON'T HAVE TO DO THAT ANYMORE!

I THINK PEOPLE UNDERESTIMATE HER SOMETIMES. SHE SEEMS QUIET AND SHY, BUT DEEP DOWN SHE'S STRONGER THAN THE REST OF US COMBINED.

HOW DO YOU KNOW WHEN A CRUSH STARTS? WHERE DOES FRIENDSHIP END AND THE CRUSH BEGIN?

IT FEELS LIKE IT SNUCK UP ON ME WHILE I WASN'T LOOKING. WHERE DID IT COME FROM AND WHY DOES IT FEEL LIKE IT'S TAKING OVER MY BRAIN?

I ASKED MY SISTER M SOME OF THESE QUESTIONS AND INSTEAD OF GIVING ME AN ANSWER SHE JUST SAID, "I DON'T KNOW? WHY? WHO DO YOU HAVE A CRUSH ON, J?"

YOU'D THINK SOMEONE WHO HAS SO MUCH EXPERIENCE WITH LOVE WOULD GIVE A BETTER ANSWER. IT'S NO SECRET SHE'S HAD A CRUSH ON A CERTAIN FOOTBALL PLAYER FOR YEARS.

WHAT I DIDN'T ASK HER WAS, WHAT DO YOU DO WHEN YOUR CRUSH ISN'T WHAT YOU EXPECTED IT WOULD BE? WHEN IT TURNS OUT THAT YOU MIGHT BE DIFFERENT THAN EVERYONE ASSUMES?

I WANT TO BELIEVE THAT IF I TOLD MY SISTERS OR MY PARENTS, IT WOULD BE OKAY. THAT THINGS WOULDN'T CHANGE. BUT I HAVE BUTTERFLIES IN MY STOMACH THAT SAY, WHAT IF IT'S NOT OKAY? WHAT WOULD I DO THEN?

SO I'M TURNING TO YOU, MY DEAR READERS, AND ASKING THIS. DO YOU HAVE A CRUSH? HOW DOES IT MAKE YOU FEEL? WHAT ARE YOU GOING TO DO WITH IT?

BECAUSE EVEN THOUGH I'VE THOUGHT ABOUT IT, AND THOUGHT ABOUT IT HARD, MY HEAD IS GIVING MY HEART NO HELP, AND I'M STUCK HERE, CONFUSED.

CAUGHT IN A CRUSHING QUANDARY,
J

WE'VE GOT OUR LATEST ISSUE!

HI, FREDDIE!

PIOP

HOT OFF THE PRESSES!

VOLCANO PRESS

VOLCANO PRESS

OH, COOL!

FINALLY!

VOLCANO

VOLCANO PRESS

I THINK IT LOOKS GREAT, IF I DO SAY SO MYSELF.

VOLCANO PRES

HAPPY VALENTINE'S DAY, GIRLS!

HAPPY VALENTINE'S DAY, MARMEE!

KNOCK
KNOCK

AND SO, IF X EQUALS THE NUMBER OF APPLES--

COME IN.

I'VE GOT CANDY-GRAAAMS!

ALL RIGHT, GO AHEAD.

groan

OOF

HEY, JO . . .

CAN WE TALK?

# CHAPTER 7

IT'S OKAY, HONEY.

IF HE'S A TRUE FRIEND, AND I THINK HE IS, HE'LL REALIZE THAT THE FRIENDSHIP YOU TWO HAVE IS MORE IMPORTANT THAN ANY CRUSH.

I DON'T THINK I CAN LIKE ANY BOY LIKE THAT.

DO YOU THINK YOU COULD GET THE OTHERS?

I THINK . . .

I THINK I'M READY TO TELL THEM.

JO!

YOU GUYS GO AHEAD. I'LL CATCH UP WITH YOU LATER.

JO, I WANTED TO APOLOGIZE TO YOU.

# CHAPTER 8

IT'S TIME TO GET UP, GIRLS.

*knock knock*

I'M TAKING BETH TO HER APPOINTMENT.

MMKAY, MARMEE

IT'S HER FINAL ROUND OF MAINTENANCE THERAPY.

OH! THAT'S TODAY!

ALL OF HER TEST RESULTS HAVE BEEN REALLY POSITIVE SO FAR.

I'LL GIVE YOU A CALL ONCE WE'VE WRAPPED THINGS UP AT THE HOSPITAL, AND YOU CAN MAKE SURE EVERYTHING HERE IS READY FOR HER.

I'VE LEFT OUT A CAKE RECIPE AND INGREDIENTS IN THE KITCHEN.

I CAN'T BELIEVE IT'S FINALLY OVER.

UH-HUH.

UH-HUH.

IT'S OFFICIAL!

BETH HAS COMPLETED HER TREATMENT!

SHE AND MARMEE ARE ON THEIR WAY HOME!

HUG

knock knock knock

WHO COULD THAT BE?

IS THAT A--?

IT'S FOR YOU, BETH. FROM MR. LAURENCE.

I LOVE IT!

RELIEF. SWEET RELIEF. THERE'S GOOD NEWS AND THEN THERE'S **GOOD** NEWS AND WE HAD TWO OF THE LATTER RECENTLY. **B** FINISHED HER TREATMENT! IT'S BEEN TWO LONG YEARS OF TESTS AND MEDICATION, AND I KNOW **B** HATED IT, AND SOMETIMES SHE DIDN'T WANT TO DO ANY OF IT, BUT NOW SHE'S FREE. SHE'S A SURVIVOR!

WE'D GOTTEN SO USED TO HER BEING SICK, OR WORRYING ABOUT HER GETTING SICK AGAIN, THAT I ALMOST DON'T KNOW WHAT TO DO WITH MYSELF. I'M TRYING TO REPLACE THE RESIDUAL WORRY WITH HAPPINESS. SEEING HER IS A DAILY REMINDER THAT I'M SO GRATEFUL SHE'S HERE.

I HAD MY OWN GOOD NEWS RECENTLY. I HAD TO BE HONEST ABOUT MYSELF TO MY FAMILY, AND IN RETURN THEY GAVE ME NOTHING BUT LOVE AND SUPPORT. I'M NOT SURE IF I'M READY TO TALK ABOUT IT HERE YET--BUT WHEN I AM, YOU'LL KNOW.

RELIEVED! RELIEVED! RELIEVED!
J

ding dong

JO! YOU'RE JUST IN TIME!

WE'RE ABOUT TO START CHARADES AND I NEED A STAR PLAYER ON MY TEAM.

AS YOU KNOW, AT THE END OF EVERY YEAR, OUR SCHOOL PUTS ON A SHOWCASE NIGHT TO HIGHLIGHT THE TALENT AND ACCOMPLISHMENTS OF OUR STUDENTS.

YOU KIDS HAVE BEEN DOING A FANTASTIC JOB.

WE'VE PUT OUT FOUR GREAT EDITIONS OF THE VOLCANO PRESS.

I DON'T KNOW IF I'VE EVER HAD SUCH A DEDICATED GROUP OF STUDENTS IN THIS CLUB.

YOU'VE ALL WORKED SO HARD.

AND EACH OF YOU HAS GROWN AND EXCELLED IN YOUR OWN WAYS.

FOR OUR FINAL EDITION, I'D LIKE TO DO SOMETHING SPECIAL.

WE'RE GOING TO HOLD AN OP-ED CONTEST. THE THEME WILL BE "WHAT I LEARNED THIS YEAR."

THE WINNING ARTICLE WILL BE SELECTED BY ME, AND BE FEATURED ON THE FRONT PAGE OF THE PAPER. THE WINNER WILL BE REVEALED AT THE END-OF-YEAR SHOWCASE.

ALL OF YOU ARE ELIGIBLE TO ENTER, BUT IT WILL MEAN EXTRA WORK. THE NEWSPAPER STILL HAS TO RUN ITS REGULAR FEATURES AND ARTICLES, SO THE CONTEST WILL BE ON TOP OF THAT.

I'M EXCITED TO SEE WHAT YOU COME UP WITH. I'D LIKE YOU TO PITCH YOUR NON-CONTEST ARTICLE IDEAS BY NEXT MEETING.

COOL!

HECK YEAH!

WATCH OUT! I'VE GOT A GREAT IDEA FOR THIS.

DAD!

MY GIRLS!

I'M SORRY IT'S BEEN SO LONG. I'VE MISSED YOU.

WE'VE MISSED YOU TOO.

MARMEE TOLD ME THE GOOD NEWS, BETH.

NO MORE CHECKUPS FOR A WHILE, HUH?

YUP.

AND JO? I'M PROUD OF YOU, HONEY.

YOUR MOM AND I LOVE YOU TREMENDOUSLY AND WILL ALWAYS SUPPORT YOU.

THANKS, DAD.

SQUEEZE

IT'S HARD TO BELIEVE THAT SUMMER IS RIGHT AROUND THE CORNER.

YOU GIRLS MUST BE EXCITED.

CAMP, BARBECUES, GOING TO THE POOL, NO MORE SCHOOL FOR TWO WHOLE MONTHS . . .

WE JUST HAVE TO GET THERE FIRST!

OH, YEAH? WHAT'S STANDING IN THE WAY?

FINAL TESTS AND PROJECTS!

NOT JUST FOR ME, BUT FOR THE KINGS TOO.

THEY WANT ME OVER THERE TUTORING ALMOST EVERY DAY.

I JUST HOPE MINNIE AND KAT DO WELL.

AND THE END-OF-YEAR SHOWCASE IS HAPPENING.

MY CLASS IS PAINTING A MURAL IN THE HALL BY THE CAFETERIA!

VERY COOL. YOU REALLY ARE MY LITTLE RAPHAEL.

MY BAND CLASS WILL BE PERFORMING THAT NIGHT TOO.

AND WE'RE PUTTING OUT THE FINAL EDITION OF THE NEWSPAPER.

SOUNDS LIKE THERE'S PLENTY TO KEEP MY KIDDOS OUT OF TROUBLE.

I'M JUST SAD I WON'T GET TO SEE IT FIRSTHAND.

WE MISS YOU, DAD!

# CHAPTER 9

242

THOMAS NILES
MIDDLE SCHOOL

END OF YEAR
SHOWCASE
TONIGHT!

I'D BETTER
GO WARM UP WITH
THE BAND!

SAW YOUR ARTICLE, BY THE WAY.

VERY COOL.

THANKS.

AH-HEH-*HEM*.

DON'T WE HAVE A MURAL TO GO SEE?

ALL RIGHT, AMY. LEAD THE WAY.

COME ON!

WAIT UP!

HEY, FREDDIE.

I JUST WANTED TO SAY CONGRATULATIONS ON WINNING THE CONTEST.

I KNEW YOU COULD DO IT.

THANKS.

I DON'T THINK I COULD HAVE DONE IT WITHOUT YOUR HELP.

THE SUGGESTIONS YOU GAVE ME REALLY MADE A DIFFERENCE.

THE WAY YOU TALKED ABOUT COMING OUT . . .

I REALLY ADMIRE YOUR HONESTY.

I THINK IT WAS PRETTY BRAVE, BEING SO OPEN LIKE THAT.

WHEN I GAVE YOU THAT FLYER BACK IN SEPTEMBER, INVITING YOU TO JOIN THE NEWSPAPER CLUB, I HAD A FEELING THERE WAS SOMETHING SPECIAL ABOUT YOU.

AND IT TURNS OUT I WAS RIGHT!

## Solving For X
### By Jo March

My name is Jo. This year I learned about Shakespeare. I learned about solving for X. I learned about electricity, and light, and countless other things in science class.

I have three sisters, and almost ever~~that phrase wi~~

I HAVE THREE SISTERS, AND ALMOST EVERYONE I MEET RESPONDS TO THAT PHRASE WITH "WHAT!? THREE!? WHAT'S THAT LIKE?"

"IT'S FINE," I USUALLY SAY, BECAUSE I DON'T HAVE ANY OTHER CONTEXT FOR IT. I SUPPOSE IT'S PROBABLY PRETTY DIFFERENT FROM BEING AN ONLY CHILD, BUT I WOULDN'T KNOW. I'VE NEVER BEEN ONE. THIS YEAR, I'VE LEARNED A LOT FROM MY SISTERS.

FROM MY OLDER SISTER, MEG, I LEARNED ABOUT PATIENCE AND PERSEVERANCE.

FROM MY YOUNGER SISTER, BETH, I LEARNED THAT HOPE IS VALUABLE, AND SHARING IT IS VITAL.

FROM MY YOUNGEST SISTER, AMY, I LEARNED ABOUT THREE-POINT PERSPECTIVE. OKAY, SO MAYBE THAT LAST ONE'S NOT VERY POETIC, BUT SOMETIMES LIFE IS LIKE THAT.

I CAME OUT IN THE MIDDLE OF THE YEAR.

I WAS KIND OF SCARED, TO BE HONEST. IT'S HARD TO BE VULNERABLE, AND THE IDEA OF COMING OUT MADE ME FEEL SMALL AND EXPOSED AND TERRIFIED.

BUT THE LONGER I WENT WITHOUT SAYING IT ALOUD, THE SMALLER AND MORE EXPOSED AND MORE TERRIFIED I FELT. UNTIL I KNEW THE ONLY WAY TO CONQUER THOSE FEELINGS WAS TO GIVE VOICE TO THAT PART OF ME.

MY NAME IS JO. THIS YEAR I LEARNED ABOUT SHAKESPEARE. I LEARNED ABOUT SOLVING FOR X. I LEARNED ABOUT ELECTRICITY, AND LIGHT, AND COUNTLESS OTHER THINGS IN SCIENCE CLASS. I ALSO LEARNED THAT I'M GAY.

I THINK WHAT SCARED ME MOST ABOUT COMING OUT WAS HOW PEOPLE WOULD REACT. I WAS SCARED MY PARENTS WOULD BE DISAPPOINTED. I WAS SCARED MY SISTERS WOULDN'T WANT TO BE AROUND ME. I WAS SCARED MY FRIENDS WOULDN'T LIKE ME ANYMORE.

BUT MY PARENTS WERE SO SUPPORTIVE--MORE SO THAN I COULD HAVE EVER IMAGINED. AND MY SISTERS TELL ME THEY WOULDN'T WANT ME ANY OTHER WAY THAN WHO I AM. AS FOR FRIENDS, WELL, THINGS WERE OKAY. AFTER A MOMENT OF EXCITEMENT, EVENTUALLY EVERYTHING WENT BACK TO NORMAL-- OR WE ALL JUST ADJUSTED TO THE NEW NORMAL? ANYWAY, REGARDLESS, I'M THANKFUL FOR EVERY SINGLE PERSON WHO HAS STOOD BY MY SIDE.

MY NAME IS JO. THIS YEAR I LEARNED ABOUT SHAKESPEARE. I LEARNED ABOUT SOLVING FOR X. I LEARNED ABOUT ELECTRICITY, AND LIGHT, AND COUNTLESS OTHER THINGS IN SCIENCE CLASS. I ALSO LEARNED THAT WE'RE ALL STRONGER THAN WE GIVE OURSELVES CREDIT FOR, AND THAT BEING KIND IS THE MOST IMPORTANT THING WE CAN BE.

# ACKNOWLEDGMENTS

Thank you to my agent, Elizabeth Bennett, for being the spark that ignited this project. Thank you to my editors, Jessica MacLeish and Alexandra Cooper, and the whole team at HC for pushing me to make my best work.

Thank you to James, Sfé, & Darren for cheering me on when I needed it, to the Wednesday-night pals at Cloudscape, and to my American friends for fielding all my questions about American vs. Canadian-isms.

And, of course, thank you to Louisa May Alcott.